BOB BARLOW'S BOOK OF

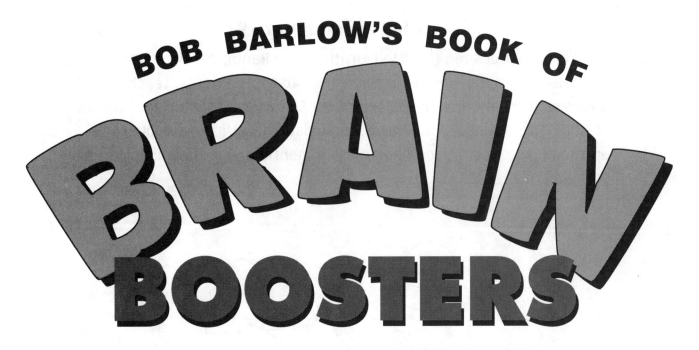

BRAIN BOOSTERS

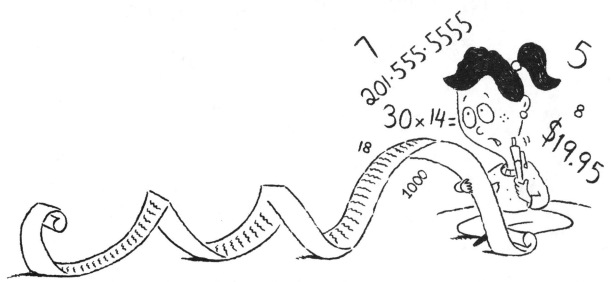

SCHOLASTIC
PROFESSIONAL BOOKS

New York ◆ Toronto ◆ London ◆ Auckland ◆ Sydney

Acknowledgments

I'd like to express my heartfelt gratitude to Randi, Ali, Julia, Mom, Mike, and the rest of my wonderful family . . . to the students, teachers, and administrators at Pine Tree Elementary School . . . to my dear friends at SUNY New Paltz . . . to Shawn Richardson and Virginia Dooley . . . and to all the people, too numerous to mention, who have inspired me throughout my life.

Cover design by Jaime Lucero and Vincent Ceci

Cover and interior art by Michael Moran

Interior design by Ellen Matlach Hassell
for Boultinghouse & Boultinghouse, Inc.

ISBN 0-590-37510-5

Dedication

This book is dedicated to creative people
everywhere—yes, that means you!

Contents

Social Studies

Critical Thinking

Introduction

"How do you throw away a garbage can?"
I couldn't have been much more than five years old when my father first asked me that question, but it's kept me thinking ever since. And although most of the activities you'll find here are a bit more complex than my dad's poser, they do share one thing in common with it: All are designed more to stimulate thought than to yield hasty "right" answers.

The value of such thought cannot be stated powerfully enough. For a long time, the popular view on creativity held that either you had it or you didn't. However, the latest brain research shows that creative "muscle," like any other, grows stronger with use. Challenge a room full of young minds every day starting in September, and you're sure to end up with a room full of higher-level thinkers come June.

And that's just what this book is all about! It contains 125 Brain Boosters: thought-provoking activities designed to engage students' minds in a variety of enjoyable ways. "Invent a system for communicating with a friend standing 100 feet away, using only the movement of your body," begins one Brain Booster. Another requires that students come up with 10 new uses for popcorn (other than eating it). Still another asks kids to ponder what would happen if every circular item in the world suddenly became a square—and every square item became circular. As you can see, Brain Boosters are by no means easy—but they are unquestionably fun.

You'll notice that I've made some of these Brain Boosters extra-easy to use by putting them in the form of full-page reproducibles. For instant creativity, just photocopy and distribute!

When should you use Brain Boosters? They're a great way to rev up those idling mental motors first thing in the morning. Or try them during transition time, to keep kids on track when they're most likely to spin out. Use them as jumping-off points for new lessons, or as centerpieces for entire units. Use them in whatever way works best for you—but for the children's sake, use them.

I've been doing precisely that for years, in my writing workshops and in my sixth-grade classroom. That's good news for you, because it has given me an opportunity to identify and fine-tune the ideas that work most effectively—and to eliminate the ones that don't. Your experiences with Brain Boosters will extend this process: I'd like to hear about what works (or doesn't work) for you, along with any questions or comments you have. You can write to me in care of Scholastic Professional Books, 555 Broadway, New York, NY 10012.

In the meantime, enjoy your students' creativity—and if you come up with a good answer to my father's question, let me know!

Language Arts

1 Invisible Poem

Open an imaginary book. Turn to page 12. Write down (or read aloud) the poem you find there.

2 Body Language

Invent a system for communicating with a friend standing 100 feet away, using only the movement of your body—no sounds allowed! Develop a vocabulary of at least 10 words.

3

Good Means, Bad Means

Do you know the difference between "good" and "bad"? Here's your chance to prove it: Write a definition of each—without using either word.

4

Sounds Like a Game

Make up a game for teaching young children the relationship between vowels and the sounds they stand for. The game can take any format you like—it could be a board game, a card game, a trivia game, or even a singing game!

5

Bow-wow Music

If dogs had a country all to themselves, what would the words to their national anthem be?

6 Sundae Theater

Do you know the details surrounding the invention of the ice cream sundae? Neither do I. But don't let that stop you: Write a one-page play about this very special moment in history.

7 Tell Me a Story

"Laura and the Purple Book" is a story that has not yet been written. In fact, you will be its author. Tell the story in brief.

8 Dear Potatoes

Write a passionate love letter . . . to your favorite food. Describe in detail why you love it so much. And please—no drooling!

9

Planet X

Clearly, something's missing here. Your job is to fill in the blanks in a way that makes sense.

I woke up _____

_____

I went to brush my teeth _____

_____

_____

I found myself on the planet Xychron _____

_____

_____

_____

_____

_____

_____

_____

_____

_____ I finished brushing my

teeth and got ready for school.

10

Why X-ray Your Zebra?

Write the longest sentence you can in which each word begins with the next letter of the alphabet—for example: "My niece, Olive, poses questions relentlessly," or "Zach and Barbara cook delicious entrees flawlessly."

11

Sing a Song of Seasons

A great composer named Vivaldi once wrote a beautiful piece of music called "The Four Seasons." Choose your favorite season and write a song about it. Just words will do for now—you can add music later, if you like. Also, feel free to illustrate your song.

12

You Will Travel the World

You have a new job: writing fortune cookie fortunes. Quick—create as many as you can in five minutes!

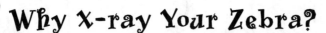

A Change for the Better

One thing is certain: Things change—sometimes for the better, sometimes for the worse. Write a children's story in which something changes in a good way—for example, a mean, stingy goat turns into a friendly, sharing goat.

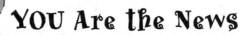

YOU Are the News

The front-page story in today's newspaper is all about you! What exactly did you do? Write the story's headline and the first three paragraphs.

How Is...?

How is your body like a factory? How is your house like a human body? How is a person like a book? Come up with answers to these questions. Then create (and answer) some "how is . . . ?" analogy questions of your own.

Change Places

What if you woke up one morning to find that you were the parent and your parents were your children? Write and stage a brief play about the possibilities.

A Really Big Book

Remember how much fun it was when, back in kindergarten, the teacher would read to you from a "big book"? Well, here's your chance to share the fun. Write a "big book" for kindergartners about one of the following topics: different kinds of weather; characteristics of trees; the letters of the alphabet; or friendship.

Book of Rhymes

You can jump real high, you can stop on a dime, but how good are you at finding a rhyme? It would be so easy if you had a place to look—so why not start yourself a rhyming book? Start keeping a rhyming dictionary today. Each day, add one "base word" (such as "and"), along with as many rhymes ("sand," "band," etc.) as you can think of.

SPECIAL DELIVERY!

19

Everybody loves to receive mail. Here's one way to ensure that you receive at least some mail—but you will have to wait awhile.

Write a letter to yourself in the future. Ask a friend or relative to send it to you in 10 years. Be sure to include information on your interests, your friends, and your plans for the future.

_____

_____

_____

_____

_____

_____

_____

_____

_____

_____

_____

_____

Please return this letter to _____

on _____ (date 10 years from now).

20 Cool Conclusions

If you've read a lot of books, you've probably noticed that some of them have super starts, matchless middles, and then—just when you're in the mood for a fantastic finale—terrible terminations. Maybe the trick is to start by writing a cool conclusion and work backward from there. Try it: Write an excellent final paragraph for a book that doesn't (yet) exist.

21 Beauty-ful Writing

Write a story that illustrates the saying, "Beauty is only skin deep."

22 First, Punch It!

Write a joke to go with this punchline: "All I can say is, he wasn't too happy with the pizza!" Write some more jokes in this way—that is, come up with a punchline first, then write the gag that leads up to it.

23

Weekend in New Jersey

The Gray Man

The Checkerboard Club

Here are three films that don't exist. But don't let that stop you—
write brief reviews of these fictional flicks. Are they great? Are
they terrible? Tell why, so I'll know whether to run to see them or
avoid them at all costs.

_____

_____

_____

_____

_____

_____

_____

_____

_____

_____

_____

_____

_____

_____

_____

_____

Three Little Nouns

Jot down three nouns on a piece of paper. Now tell a brief story that ties them all together.

An Alien Message

You have only 100 words to tell an alien race everything you can about humans. Get to it!

A Meaningful Task

The editors of a new dictionary need you to carry out a very important task: Come up with never-before-heard words for the definitions below. When you're finished, think of some other things for which there are no words and invent words for them.

_____: The phenomenon in which two people start talking at the exact same time, then stop, then once again start talking at the same time.

_____: Thinking that you see someone you know, calling out his or her name—then realizing it's not the person you thought it was.

_____: Continuing to argue with someone even after you've realized that you're completely wrong.

_____

_____

_____

_____

_____

_____

_____

_____

_____

_____

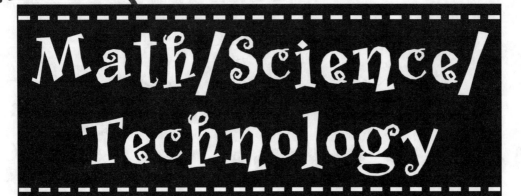

Math/Science/ Technology

27 Thoughts Add Up

How many thoughts do you have in a day? Devise a method to answer this question.

28 A Safe Way to Go

Cars can be a great way to get from one place to another. But sometimes they can be dangerous. Draw and describe your design for the world's safest car.

Tree Count

Devise a plan for determining how many trees there are in the world.

Paper Puzzler

Make the most amazing thing you can, using five pieces of loose-leaf paper.

A Frozen Question

Without using artificial refrigerants, how would you keep a snowperson from melting through the summer?

32

1,098,745,951

Come up with a foolproof way to remember the number 1,098,745,951, and do it. No paper or pencils allowed—just that great mind of yours!

33

Inventomania

Create as many inventions as you can using string, a coin with a hole in it, a marble, a cup of water, a magnifying glass, and a tape recorder.

34

Sit and Think About It

List all the things you can do with a chair other than sit on it. Illustrate your ideas.

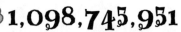

35 The Next Million

Most scientists agree that life on Earth has evolved, or changed gradually, over millions of years. Where do you believe evolution will take humans over the next million years? Answer in words and pictures.

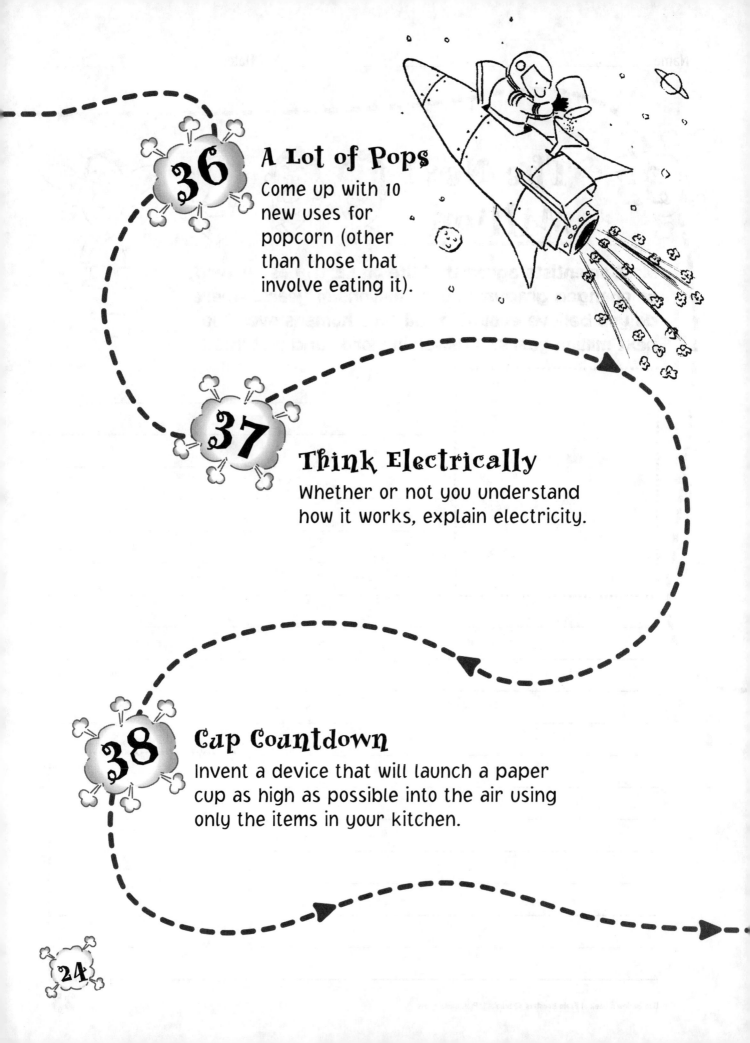

36 A Lot of Pops

Come up with 10 new uses for popcorn (other than those that involve eating it).

37 Think Electrically

Whether or not you understand how it works, explain electricity.

38 Cup Countdown

Invent a device that will launch a paper cup as high as possible into the air using only the items in your kitchen.

Name _____ Date _____

Daily Count

Make a list of everything you did yesterday that had anything to do with numbers.

_____
_____
_____
_____
_____
_____
_____
_____
_____
_____
_____
_____
_____
_____
_____

40

Geometry Dance

The Geometry Dance involves squares, triangles, circles, and many other shapes. How do I know? I just made it up! Your job is to choreograph and perform this never-before-seen dance.

41

You Talk Too Much

How many people have you spoken to in your life? Devise a reasonable way to answer this question.

42

Fruity Calculations

List all the math ideas you could teach using a gallon container of fruit salad. Explain how you would teach each one.

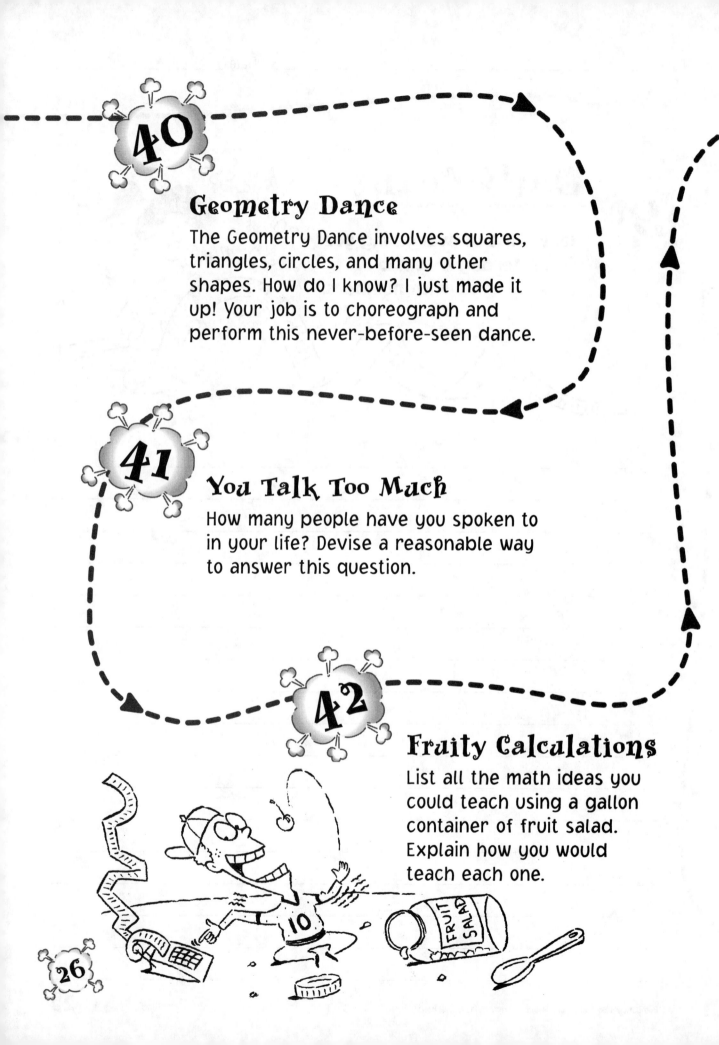

43 It's a Wonderful Leaf

Can a single leaf falling from a tree to the ground have an effect on the world? What are some possible effects?

44 Ketchup by the Gallon

Develop a plan to determine how much ketchup (or mustard, if you're not a ketchup fan) you have eaten in your life.

45 Changing Shapes

What would happen if every circular item in the world suddenly became a square— and every square became a circle?

46 Blue Skies

Give three absolutely ridiculous, laughably false explanations for the sky being blue. (You may already know that the sky's blue hue results from the way molecules in the atmosphere interact with the sun's light, but forget about that for now.)

47 Kiddie Count

Write a poem designed to teach pre-school children how to count from 1 to 10. And stay away from the old "one, two, buckle my shoe" stuff—use your creativity to come up with something completely new.

48 If You Could Build a Better Pillow

With all the amazing technologies we have nowadays, one truly astounding fact is that the pillow has not changed much over the years. It will now, though: Design the pillow of the future and write about all the wonderful functions of which it is capable.

Numerous Personalities

49

Imagine that the numbers 1 to 10 are people. How would they behave? Which number would be the smartest? the funniest? the laziest? the nicest? the ugliest? Write brief personality sketches of each number.

1 _____

_____

2 _____

_____

3 _____

_____

4 _____

_____

5 _____

_____

6 _____

_____

7 _____

_____

8 _____

_____

9 _____

_____

10 _____

_____

50 More than Right Angles

Write an entertaining story designed to teach first graders about the differences and similarities between squares and rectangles.

51 Past or Future?

You have one hour to spend in the past or the future. To what year would you go, and what would you do there?

52 Predict the Unpredictable

Dream up a new invention. Write what it does. Then write something completely unpredictable that it might do.

53 If I Had $10,000

You may have heard the saying, "It takes money to make money." Assume you have $10,000 to work with. How would you use it to make more money?

54 Float or Fly?

Look around your room. Using only the materials available there, which would be easier to construct—a boat or a hang-glider? Choose one, then draw and describe how you would go about making it.

55 Flat Facts

The Pancake Theory

Did you know that some people still believe that Earth is flat? Whether or not you agree with this theory, come up with as much evidence as you can to support it.

56

Answer with a Bang

How would you use the items in your classroom to make the loudest possible sound? Describe and illustrate your answer.

57

Odds versus Evens

Create the story of "The Battle Between the Odd and Even Numbers." (Remember that odd and even numbers have some interesting qualities. Add two evens and you get another even. Add two odds and you still get an even. Add an odd and an even and you end up with an odd. That **is** odd . . .)

58

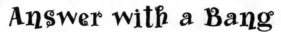

A Hatful of Surprises

Design a hat that is capable of at least three surprising functions (beyond those already associated with hats). Be sure to illustrate and describe your super hat's amazing capabilities.

Personal Logo

Using only triangles, circles, and squares, create a logo or symbol that represents you. Write a brief explanation of your creation.

_____

_____

_____

_____

_____

_____

_____

_____

_____

60

Once upon a Prime...

Develop a story that can be used to teach the concept of prime and composite numbers to seven-year-olds. As you no doubt know, a prime number is one that is divisible only by itself and the number 1.

61

Chew on It

Quick—come up with (and illustrate) as many new uses for chewing gum as you can. And if you feel like giving up, don't—stick with it! (Sorry!)

62

Star Stories

Nowadays we know that the stars we see are incandescent spheres of burning gas, similar to our own sun. But it wasn't too long ago that people thought otherwise. What are some possible alternative explanations for the existence of these flickering points of light in the night sky?

It's Alarming

63

Invent a device that will wake you up in the morning, using any (or all) of the following materials and one additional item of your choosing (if necessary). Draw and describe your invention.

empty
milk carton

soccer ball

water

string

magnifying glass

brick

_____

_____

_____

_____

_____

_____

_____

_____

Social Studies

64 Choose Wisely

If you could have only two of the following—wealth, intelligence, and friends—which two would you choose? Why?

65 Future Fashion

Think about (or conduct some research on) how people dressed 300, 200, and 100 years ago. Then, draw and describe the kind of clothing and accessories people will be wearing 100, 200, and 300 years from now.

66 Budget Carefully

Let's say there's just enough money to pay for three of the following five things: education, space exploration, the arts, the military, and the environment. Which three would you choose, and why would you choose these over the others?

67 Design for Learning

What if you were given the opportunity to redesign your school from scratch? How would it be different physically? What kinds of classes would be taught? In what ways would you improve the school?

68 Your Place in the World

What kind of impact have you had on the world? You may not think you've had much of an impact at all . . . but if you think about it, you'll realize that just about everything you do affects other people. For example, someone who's having a lousy day might see your smile and brighten up. A little bit of that good feeling will rub off on the next person he or she meets. You get the picture. So answer the question: In what ways have you had an impact on the world?

69 Personal Pennant

The flag of the United States of America includes a number of symbols that tell a story about our country. The stars each stand for a different state, while the thirteen stripes represent the original colonies. Draw a flag that uses symbols to tell a number of important things about you. Explain the meaning of each symbol.

70 Weapons for Peace

There's a verse in the Bible that talks about beating "swords into ploughshares"—in other words, turning weapons of war into implements of peace. Think of some weapons and write about how you would turn them into peaceful hardware.

71 Town of the Future

Draw a picture of your town as you imagine it will look in 100 years. How will the streets and sidewalks be different? The stores and other businesses? The schools and homes? The parks and playgrounds?

72 Friendship Recipe

Write a recipe for friendship.
As with any recipe, include the
necessary ingredients and
describe what must be done with
them to achieve the desired result.

FRIENDSHIP

Ingredients:

_____

_____

_____

_____

Directions:

_____

_____

_____

_____

_____

_____

_____

_____

_____

_____

73 The Mnemonic Earth

Develop a mnemonic device for remembering the names of the Great Lakes, the world's oceans, or the seven continents.

74 A New Way to Say "Hey"

It's time to shake the dust off the old handshake. Develop a new greeting to replace it. Describe this new greeting and explain why it's better than a handshake.

75 You Can Change the World

Make a list of all the things you can personally do to make the world a better place. Choose one—and do it!

Freedom Is...

76 Everybody talks about freedom.
Our country was built on the
idea of freedom for all. But what is
freedom? Define freedom in your own
words. Then draw an original symbol that
means freedom to you.

FREEDOM IS:

Freedom is _____

_____

_____

_____

_____

_____

_____

| FREEDOM |

77 Careful Consideration

Which is more important: taking care of yourself or taking care of others? Don't just answer the question—defend your response in such a way as to convince whoever hears it that you are right.

78 Dig for an Idea

Centuries from now, archaeologists make an amazing find: your room! How might they misinterpret what they discover? What, for instance, would they make of your posters, CDs, books, musical instruments, sports equipment, and all your other "stuff"?

Wisdom of Generations

In some cultures, family wisdom is passed down from generation to generation as a matter of course. Pass down some of the wisdom you have accumulated, in a brief letter to your children and grandchildren.

Dear _____,

_____

_____

_____

_____

_____

_____

_____

_____

_____

_____

_____

_____

_____,

_____

_____

80

Fad of the Future

Five years from now, a new
craze will sweep the nation.
Everybody will be doing it.
What is it?

81

How to Save the World

There is an old saying that goes roughly like
this: "If you save a single life, it is just as if
you had saved the entire world." What does
this saying mean?

Critical Thinking

82 Make Another Holiday

Invent a new holiday. What does this holiday celebrate? What is it called? What songs are sung on this day, what food is eaten, and what kinds of activities take place?

83 What Do You Know About Snow?

Describe snow to someone who has never seen it. Use as many senses as possible to express what you have to say: Consider the look, feel, taste, sound, and even the smell of snow. If you've never seen snow, describe rain instead.

84 Consider the Options

Which punishment would be worse: never again seeing the color red or never again seeing your favorite cable channel?

85 Your Own Game

Invent a game that uses only the following things: five small stones, a smooth wooden surface, a cup of sand, and your creativity.

86 Homemade Rhythm

Using only the items in your desk, create a percussion instrument. When you and your classmates have completed your instruments, improvise a brief percussion piece.

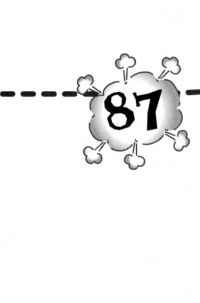

87 Do You Lack Sense?

If you had to live for one year without three of your senses, which two would you choose to keep? Why?

88 Cold Complaints

The items in your refrigerator have gone on strike and posted a list of demands (right next to the mustard). What are their demands?

89 Rainbow's End

You see a rainbow . . . you decide to follow it to its end . . . once there, you find not a pot of gold but something even more amazing and wonderful . . . what is it? Write and illustrate the story of "What's Really at the End of the Rainbow."

90 Birthday Mystery

You pick up a wrapped birthday present and shake it. First it rings. Then it gets heavier. Finally it starts to smell like the forest after a heavy rainstorm. Come up with an explanation for this apparently inexplicable sequence of events.

91 Colorless Conversation

Turn to the person next to you and have a two-minute discussion about how the world would be different if there were no colors other than black and white.

92 The Short and Tall of It

List five advantages of being extra tall and five advantages of being extra short.

93

Psssssst...

I know your secret: You aren't really you. You're a superhero with amazing powers. What are they? What's your name? Where are you originally from? What does your costume look like? What's your secret hangout like? How did you get your superpowers? Anything else you'd like to tell us . . . ?

_____

_____

_____

_____

_____

_____

_____

_____

_____

_____

_____

_____

_____

_____

_____

_____

_____

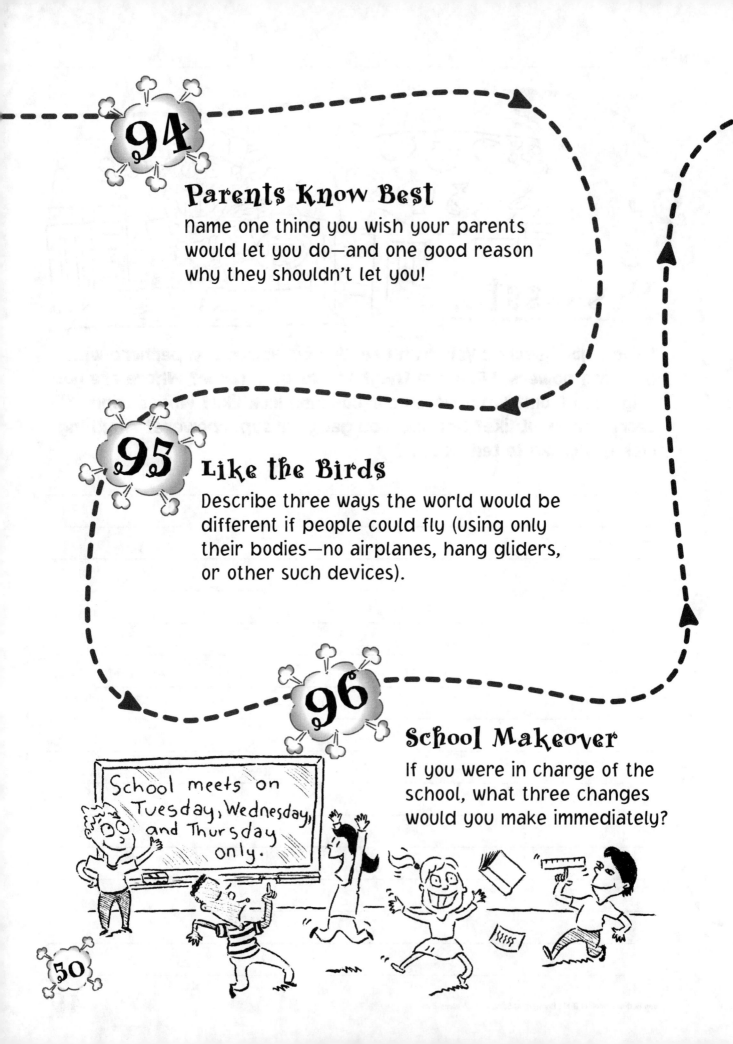

94 Parents Know Best

Name one thing you wish your parents would let you do—and one good reason why they shouldn't let you!

95 Like the Birds

Describe three ways the world would be different if people could fly (using only their bodies—no airplanes, hang gliders, or other such devices).

96 School Makeover

If you were in charge of the school, what three changes would you make immediately?

School meets on Tuesday, Wednesday, and Thursday only.

97 Same Old Song

The song "Happy Birthday" is well known to us all, but let's face it: This old tune has had a few too many birthdays itself. So . . . your job is to write the new birthday song!

98 Stop the Clock

Imagine that you can stop time for a period of 10 seconds. How would you put this ability to use? In what ways might it be a disadvantage?

99 Colorful Moods

Think of the colors of the rainbow. List each one, and next to it write how it makes you feel. Then write a poem about the colors and the emotions you associate with them.

 100 Future Views

Some people think it would be nice to be able to see the future. But there might be some problems with clairvoyance. What do you think they might be?

101 Artistic Cooperation

Working in groups of four, simultaneously create four "assembly line drawings." Here's how:

1. Each person draws a head. The drawings are passed to the right.
2. Everybody now draws a torso. Drawings rotate again.
3. Arms and legs are drawn in.
4. After a final rotation, add "extras" such as earrings, facial hair, and glasses.

102 Body Language

Express the following emotions through body language alone— no facial expressions allowed: happiness, sadness, surprise, anger, confusion, boredom, curiosity, and shock.
Remember: Keep a poker face.

103

Thoughts for Your Penny

Imagine that the U.S. Mint needs new designs for pennies, nickels, dimes, and quarters—and you have been chosen to create them. Get to it—and don't forget that every coin has an "obverse" and a "reverse" (also known as a front and a back).

Penny

Nickel

Dime

Quarter

104 A Different Birthday Gift

You have told all of your friends and relatives that you don't want any money or presents for your next birthday. What would you like instead?

105 Broken Promises

Make a list of all the things that can result from breaking a promise.

106 Act Like an Animal

Consider the (nonhuman) animals you are familiar with. Think about how they behave. Is there anything we can learn from them? Are there any ways it would benefit us to behave more like them?

Metamorphosis

A caterpillar weaves a chrysalis and emerges as a butterfly. Imagine weaving your own chrysalis. What would you be when you emerged?

108 Mirror, Mirror

Before there were mirrors, it wasn't easy for people to know how they looked to the rest of the world. Now that mirrors are plentiful, though, we have come to take them for granted. Make a list of the things you can do with a mirror—and try to think up some new uses.

109 The Secret Lives of Cats and Dogs

Dogs and cats have a secret they've been keeping from us for years. What is it?

110 Can You See Me?

Imagine that you can make yourself invisible. What are some ways you might use this power? What are some ways it might backfire?

111 Shrink Power

Imagine that you can shrink yourself down to the size of a dime. Can you think of some advantages to having this ability? Can you think of any disadvantages?

112 Deep Thoughts

In what ways do you think your life might be different if you and your family lived underground?

Name _____   Date _____

Sweet Inspiration

113

Invent a new candy bar. Include the treat's ingredients, its name, an illustration of its cross section, and a design for a wrapper.

Candy Bar Name: _____

Ingredients: _____

_____

_____

_____

_____

_____

_____

cross section

candy bar wrapper design

114 Draw from the Heart

Using a pencil and paper, draw your impression of the following emotions: happiness, sadness, surprise, anger, confusion, boredom, curiosity, and shock. Try to stay away from smiles, frowns, words, and other conventional symbols of feelings.

115 Three in One

Invent a new game that combines elements of at least three other games (baseball, hockey, and checkers, for instance, or chess, football, and archery).

116 Dream Room

Describe and illustrate your "perfect room." What kinds of things would be in it? How would the room be arranged? What would the view from the window be? How would the room be shaped? Be as detailed as possible in your answer.

117 Terrific Me

Write down as many wonderful things about yourself as you can. Don't be shy about it—just tell the truth about what a terrific person you are!

118 Shocking Thoughts

How was life different before electricity? Think about how you use electricity every day—and about how your life would change without it.

119 Just One Bite

Describe (and illustrate) the grossest sandwich you can imagine. Be sure to include a full list of all the disgusting ingredients!

120

Be Fair About it

Do "fair" and "equal" mean the same thing? Explain your answer.

121

Boost Your Brain Power

Bodybuilders use weights to develop bigger muscles. How do "brain builders" develop bigger mental muscles? Design the ultimate workout for your mind.

122

Uncommon Sense

How would you describe colors to someone who has never seen? How would you describe sounds to someone who has never heard? How would you describe tastes to someone born without taste buds? How would you describe smells to someone born without a sense of smell? How would you describe the tactile sense (feeling) to someone who has no sense of touch? Choose one of these questions and answer it.

Design for Future Fun

Describe and illustrate the sport of the future in as much detail as possible. Include rules, playing area, uniforms, and anything else that might help the reader understand the sport.

Sport: _____

Rules: _____

_____

_____

_____

_____

_____

_____

_____

_____

_____

124 Past or Future

Which would you rather have: a camera that could take pictures of the past or a dog that could smell the future?

125 Tell the Truth

Is it ever okay to lie?
If so, when?
If not, why not?

Name _____ Date _____

Goals for a Lifetime

It has been said that going through life without goals is a little bit like trying to find hidden treasure without a map. Set one goal for yourself for each of the following.

Today's Goal: _____

_____

This Week's Goal: _____

_____

This Month's Goal: _____

_____

This Year's Goal: _____

_____

_____

This Decade's Goal: _____

_____

My Lifetime Goal: _____

_____

_____

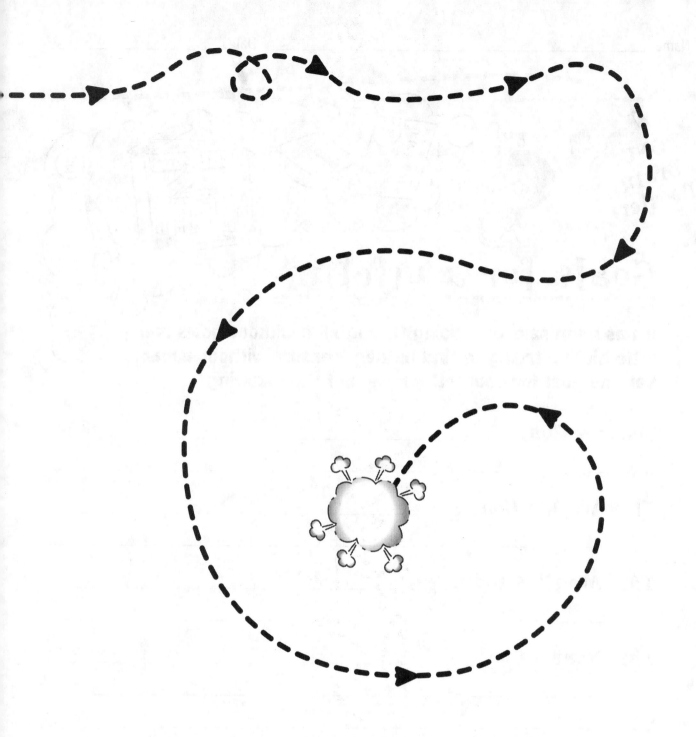